Here Is Big Bunny

Steve Henry

I Like to Read®

HOLIDAY HOUSE • NEW YORK

I Like to Read® books, created by award-winning
picture book artists as well as talented newcomers,
instill confidence and the joy of reading in new readers.

We want to hear every new reader say, "I like to read!"

Visit our website for flash cards, activities, and more about the series:
www.holidayhouse.com/I-Like-to-Read/
#ILTR
This book has been tested by an educational expert
and determined to be a guided reading level A.

I LIKE TO READ® is a registered trademark of Holiday House Publishing, Inc.
Copyright © 2016 by Steve Henry
All Rights Reserved
HOLIDAY HOUSE is registered in the U.S. Patent and Trademark Office.
Printed and bound in April 2017 at Hong Kong Graphics and Printing Ltd., China.
The artwork was drawn in ink and painted with watercolor, gouache, and
acrylic paintings on hot pressed watercolor paper.
www.holidayhouse.com
1 3 5 7 9 10 8 6 4 2
Library of Congress Cataloging-in-Publication Data
Henry, Steve, 1948-
Here Is Big Bunny / Steve Henry. — First edition.
pages cm.
Summary: Baffling sightings in a busy city—an ear behind a tall building, a nose outside a
fancy store, a bushy tail in the park,
a foot outside the museum, and more—provide clues to the true identity of Big Bunny.
ISBN 978-0-8234-3458-9 (hardcover)
[1. Rabbits—Fiction. 2. Size—Fiction.] I. Title.
PZ7.H39732He 2016
[E]—dc23
2014048571

ISBN 978-0-8234-3885-3 (paperback)

For Mary, my very first friend

Here is a foot.

Here is a foot.

Here is a hand.

Here is a hand.

Here is a tail.

Here is a tail.

Here is an ear.

Here is an ear.

Here are ears.

Here is an eye.

Here is an eye.

Here is a nose.

Here is a nose.

Here is a face.

Here is a face.

Here is Big Bunny.

Here is Big Bunny.

I Like to Read®

Visit http://www.holidayhouse.com/I-Like-to-Read/ **for more about I Like to Read®
books, including flash cards, reproducibles, and the complete list of titles.**